This Little Tiger book belongs to:

_____

_____

_____

For Charlotte, with all my love xx ~ T. C.

For my cousin Felicity ~ A. E.

LITTLE TIGER PRESS LTD,
an imprint of the Little Tiger Group
1 Coda Studios, 189 Munster Road, London SW6 6AW
www.littletiger.co.uk

First published in Great Britain 2012
This edition published 2020
Text copyright © Tracey Corderoy 2012, 2020
Illustrations copyright © Alison Edgson 2012
Tracey Corderoy and Alison Edgson have asserted their rights to be identified as the
author and illustrator of this work under the Copyright, Designs and Patents Act, 1988
A CIP catalogue record for this book is available from the British Library

LTP/2700/3269/0620 • ISBN 978-1-78881-830-8
Manufactured, printed, and assembled in Foshan, China. First printing, June 2020
2 4 6 8 10 9 7 5 3 1

Just One More!

by

Tracey Corderoy

Illustrated by

Alison Edgson

LITTLE TIGER

LONDON

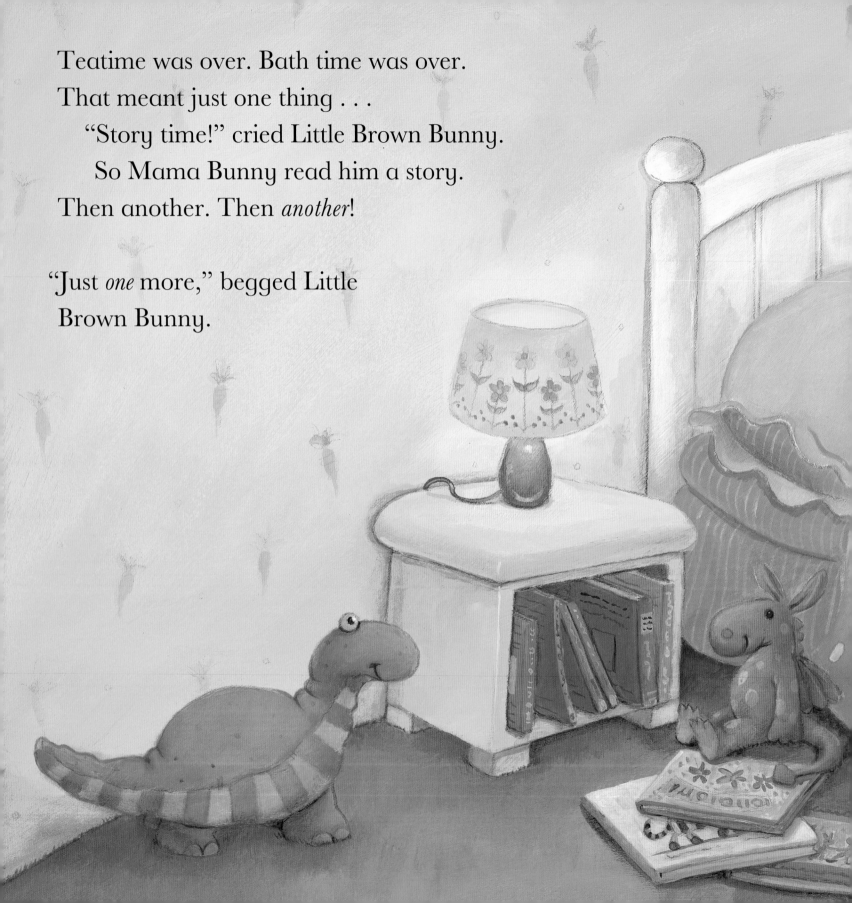

Teatime was over. Bath time was over.
That meant just one thing . . .
   "Story time!" cried Little Brown Bunny.
   So Mama Bunny read him a story.
Then another. Then *another*!

"Just *one* more," begged Little
Brown Bunny.

So Papa read him one more
story, right to the end.
    Still Bunny said, "Just one more?"
    "Granny's turn!" cried Papa
Rabbit.

When Granny had read *all* the dragon books,

and Grandpa had read them *again*, Little Brown Bunny still wanted . . . "Just one more!"

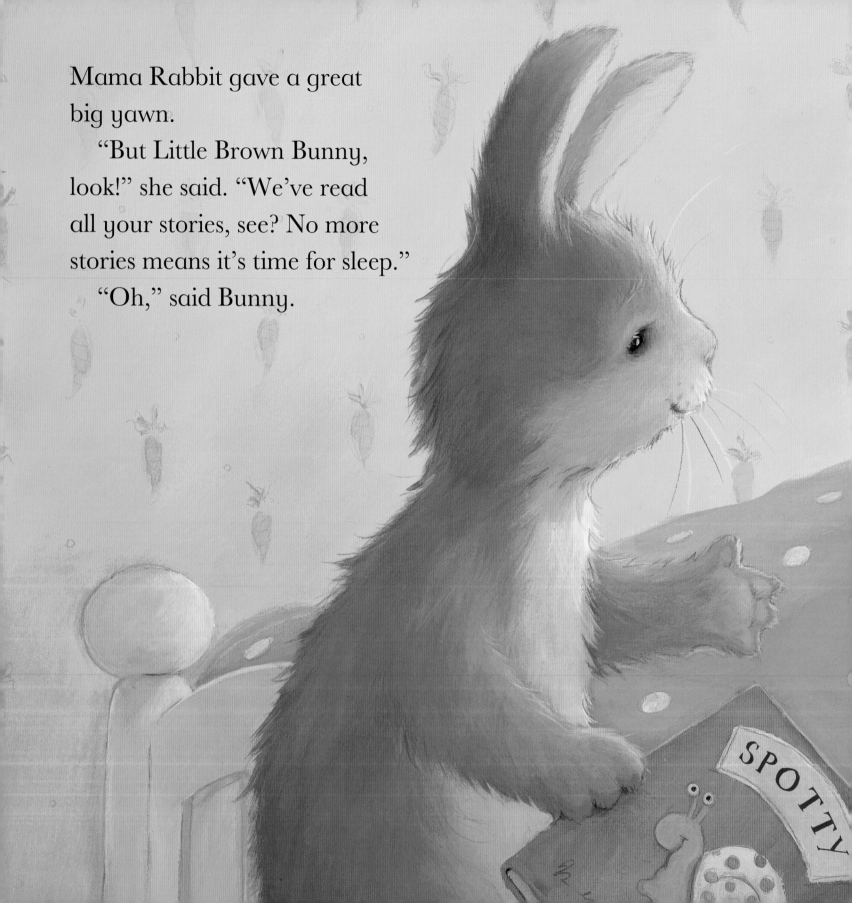

Mama Rabbit gave a great big yawn.

"But Little Brown Bunny, look!" she said. "We've read all your stories, see? No more stories means it's time for sleep."

"Oh," said Bunny.

"Maybe," he whispered,
"I'll *make* a bedtime book.
A super, super-long one!
Then story time will last
all night."

Next morning Bunny hopped out of bed.
"Hooray!" he cried. "Time to make
my story."

He bounced across to his making-things box.
Soon he was writing big, long words and
drawing lots of pictures.

At last, he heaved up his heavy book.
This was going to be the longest
story *ever*!

"Are you sitting comfortably?"
he asked his toys. "We might be here
a long, long time!"

Two minutes later, it was all over.
"Oh-h-h!" sighed Bunny.
"My super-long story wasn't
super-long at all."

"Don't worry," said Mama Bunny. "Why don't you go and ask your friends what stories *they* like? Then you can add them to your book."

"You're so clever!" cried Little Brown Bunny, and off he went.

CARROT COTTAGE

Little Owl was playing with his rocket
when Bunny bounced in.

"The stories *I* like best," Owl hooted, "are
ones about the moooooon! One day I'm
going to fly there! Zooooom!"

"I love the moon, too!" said Bunny.
"Thanks, Owl!"
    And he blasted off to find Little Mouse . . .

Little Mouse was having a teeny snack when Bunny bounded in. "I love stories about cheese!" she mumbled. "Big cheese, small cheese, round cheese, smelly cheese – *any* cheese really!"

"Thanks, Mouse!" giggled Bunny, holding his nose. And he raced off to find Little Wolf . . .

Little Wolf was having a tea party when Bunny came by.

"Well, I do love stories about piggies!" he said. "And that grandma with the big, furry ears!"

"The story *I* like," grinned Big Papa Wolf, "is the one all about . . ."

"Hugs!"

"Oh, Papa," giggled
Little Wolf, "what big
arms you have!"
"All the better to hug
you with!" chuckled
Papa Wolf. And
he gave his boy
a big Papa kiss
on the nose.

"Thanks for your help," Bunny
called. Then he huffed and puffed
all the way back home!

Little Brown Bunny got out his book and scribbled down stories of moons made of cheese, and rockets and big, fluffy hugs.

By the time he had finished, it was dark outside.

"Come on, everyone!" he called. "This is going to be the best, most super-duper storybook *ever!*"

He opened it ever so
carefully and took a big,
deep breath. Then Little
Brown Bunny . . .

. . . fell fast asleep!